Teen Activism LIBRARY

STAND UP
for LGBTQ Rights

Don Nardo

San Diego, CA

© 2022 ReferencePoint Press, Inc.
Printed in the United States

For more information, contact:
ReferencePoint Press, Inc.
PO Box 27779
San Diego, CA 92198
www.ReferencePointPress.com

ALL RIGHTS RESERVED.
No part of this work covered by the copyright hereon may be reproduced or used in any form or by any means—graphic, electronic, or mechanical, including photocopying, recording, taping, web distribution, or information storage retrieval systems—without the written permission of the publisher.

LIBRARY OF CONGRESS CATALOGING-IN-PUBLICATION DATA

Names: Nardo, Don, 1947- author.
Title: Stand up for LGBTQ rights / Don Nardo.
Description: San Diego : ReferencePoint Press, 2021. | Series: Teen
  activism library | Includes bibliographical references and index.
Identifiers: LCCN 2021013186 (print) | LCCN 2021013187 (ebook) | ISBN
  9781678201524 (library binding) | ISBN 9781678201531 (ebook)
Subjects: LCSH: Sexual minorities--United States--Juvenile literature. |
  Sexual minorities--Legal status, laws, etc.--United States--Juvenile
  literature. | Gay rights--United States--Juvenile literature. | Sex and
  law--United States--Juvenile literature.
Classification: LCC HQ73.3.U6 N37 2021 (print) | LCC HQ73.3.U6 (ebook) |
  DDC 306.760973--dc23
LC record available at https://lccn.loc.gov/2021013186
LC ebook record available at https://lccn.loc.gov/2021013187

CONTENTS

Introduction   4
Willing to Stand Up for Justice and Equality

Chapter One   8
The Issue Is LGBTQ Rights

Chapter Two   19
The Activists

Chapter Three   30
The Teen Activist's Tool Kit

Chapter Four   41
Risks and Rights

Source Notes   52
Where to Go for Ideas and Inspiration   56
Index   59
Picture Credits   63
About the Author   64

INTRODUCTION

Willing to Stand Up for Justice and Equality

"I am very happy to see justice prevail, after spending almost my entire high school career fighting for equal treatment,"[1] nineteen-year-old Drew Adams stated on August 7, 2020. A recent graduate of Allen D. Nease High School in Ponte Vedra, Florida, Adams had just won a resounding victory in a court case that centered on his basic civil rights. While attending his high school, he had simply wanted to use the boys' restrooms like all other boys. However, school officials, including members of the local school board, had forbade him from doing so. Their argument was that he should be excluded because he was trans (short for *transgender*, meaning he had transitioned his gender from female to male). Although never said explicitly, the inference was that Adams's entry into a boys' restroom posed some sort of threat to other boys.

Adams had countered that he was no threat to anyone. Rather, he simply wanted to be treated like other boys. "High school is hard enough," he said after winning the case, "without having your school separate you from your peers and mark you as inferior. I hope this decision helps save other transgender students from having to go through that painful and humiliating experience."[2]

The judges who ruled in favor of Adams certainly sent that message of hope to other trans youth. In their decision, they held that preventing trans students from using the restrooms that match their gender is unconstitutional. The reason, the judges ruled, is because such exclusion based on sex violates the equal protection clause of the US Constitution's Fourteenth Amendment. According to the judges,

> "High school is hard enough without having your school separate you from your peers."[2]
>
> —Drew Adams, an activist in Florida

> Workplace discrimination against transgender people is contrary to law. Neither should this discrimination be tolerated in schools. The School Board's bathroom policy, as applied to Mr. Adams, singled him out for different treatment because of his transgender status. . . . A public school may not punish its students for gender nonconformity. Neither may a public school harm transgender students by establishing arbitrary, separate rules for their restroom use.[3]

Standing Up for Themselves

By taking his high school and school board to court, Adams became one of several members of the LGBTQ community to engage in overt activism to stand up for himself and secure his fundamental rights. He and other trans people represent the *T* in *LGBTQ*. That well-known abbreviation incorporates various aspects of sexual orientation and gender identity. The *L* stands for *lesbian*, for example, the *G* for *gay*, and the *B* for *bisexual*, frequently shortened to *bi*. Meanwhile, the *Q*, most often meaning *queer*, was added to the traditional acronym *LGBT* during the 1990s. The Center, an influential LGBTQ advocacy organization, explains that the term *queer*, which used to be a derogatory slur against gay people, has come to be used in a more positive way,

Drew Adams, a transgender teen, speaks to reporters after winning his lawsuit against school officials in Ponte Vedra, Florida, who had prohibited him from using the boys' restroom.

especially by younger LGBTQ people. They feel that their "sexual orientation is not exclusively heterosexual." To them, "the terms lesbian, gay, and bisexual are perceived to be too limiting."[4]

Whether they are gay, trans, or queer, in recent decades a growing number of young people from the LGBTQ community have become social activists fighting for equal rights and treatment. Some, such as Adams, have taken their cases to court. Others have opted for different forms of activism, including writing articles for newspapers and social media platforms, starting LGBTQ clubs in their schools, and expressing their sexual orientation or gender identity through theater, film, and other arts.

In whatever manner they choose to stand up for themselves, all of these young activists have the same basic motivation: achieving equal rights for LGBTQ people, who still are not always accorded equal treatment and respect. In schools across the United States, for instance, LGBTQ students continue to be bullied and sometimes even physically attacked. Most high schools still do not teach about the history and struggles of the LGBTQ community, and in some high schools and colleges, LGBTQ people are excluded from sports teams. Furthermore, many politicians continue to try to keep these individuals out of the military, and undetermined numbers of LGBTQ people endure discrimination in the workplace.

Willing to Challenge the System

Most older LGBTQ people grew up in an era in which such discrimination was deeply ingrained in society. As a result, most of them did not "come out" publicly, or even to their families, until fairly recently, if at all. In contrast, many younger members of the LGBTQ community refuse to buckle under to ignorance, hatred, and discrimination. They tend to be open about who they are and are willing to challenge and change the system.

Typical of the newest generations of LGBTQ folk is Ethan Collier-Moreno, a gay high school senior from San Diego, California. Growing up, he says, "I was exposed to more conservative points of view. Racism, homophobia, transphobia, and various issues plague the community [I] grew up in. Attending school . . . I've seen the true struggles of students in their education and especially the struggle LGBTQ students face within [my] school district."[5]

Appalled by these injustices, Ethan felt he could not simply stand by and do nothing about them. So, he boldly ran for and won a seat on the California Association of Student Councils, a nonprofit group that advocates for the welfare of students statewide. "I have and will always be," he states, "a lifelong advocate for education reform, gender equality, youth civic engagement and most importantly, LGBTQ human rights."[6] Ethan Collier-Moreno and Drew Adams are two of many young LGBTQ people who are standing up for their rights.

> "I've seen the true struggles of students in their education."[5]
>
> —Ethan Collier-Moreno, an activist in California

CHAPTER ONE

The Issue Is LGBTQ Rights

Mark was born with the body of a female, and his parents named him Marcy. He recalls, however, that he knew from an early age that something about his gender was not right. He felt that on the inside he was really a boy who somehow had ended up in the wrong body.

Years later, the diagnosis of a physician indicated that Mark, now in his teens, had been right. Indeed, the doctor explained, because of a complex set of chemical and hormonal interactions that occurred when he was in his mother's womb, he was born transgender—with the body of a girl but the brain and gender identity of a boy. Trying to alleviate the situation, in his twenties Mark underwent a physical transition from female to male, which included the need to take appropriate hormones on a regular basis.

At first, Mark did not tell anyone outside his family that he was trans, mainly because he feared that people would reject or discriminate against him. Once more, he turned out to be right. When he was in his thirties, he decided to go ahead and be honest with people about who he was. One consequence was that when he moved to a small town in Iowa in 2016, he needed to find a new doctor to prescribe his hormones. There was a physician who specialized in hormone treatments in a hospital 40 miles (64 km) away. The problem, Mark explains, was that the hospital director "did not allow any of her physicians to prescribe hormones to trans people. Instead, she forced people like me to go to doctors in Iowa City, a ninety-mile drive one way."[7]

Exasperated, Mark took the hospital to mediation, a form of dispute resolution outside of law courts. "They showed up with a force meant to intimidate me," he says. "There was an attorney, the doctor, and two other people whose presence seemed entirely irrelevant. I did not have an attorney or any other representation. Needless to say, they wouldn't budge."[8]

Widespread Anti-LGBTQ Discrimination

Mark adds that he knows he is not the only trans person to suffer from discrimination in health care. Backing him up was a major 2017 national survey by the Center for American Progress, a noted nonpartisan public policy research organization headquartered in Washington, DC. It found that 29 percent, or almost a third, of those interviewed said that a doctor or other health care provider had refused to treat them solely because they were trans.

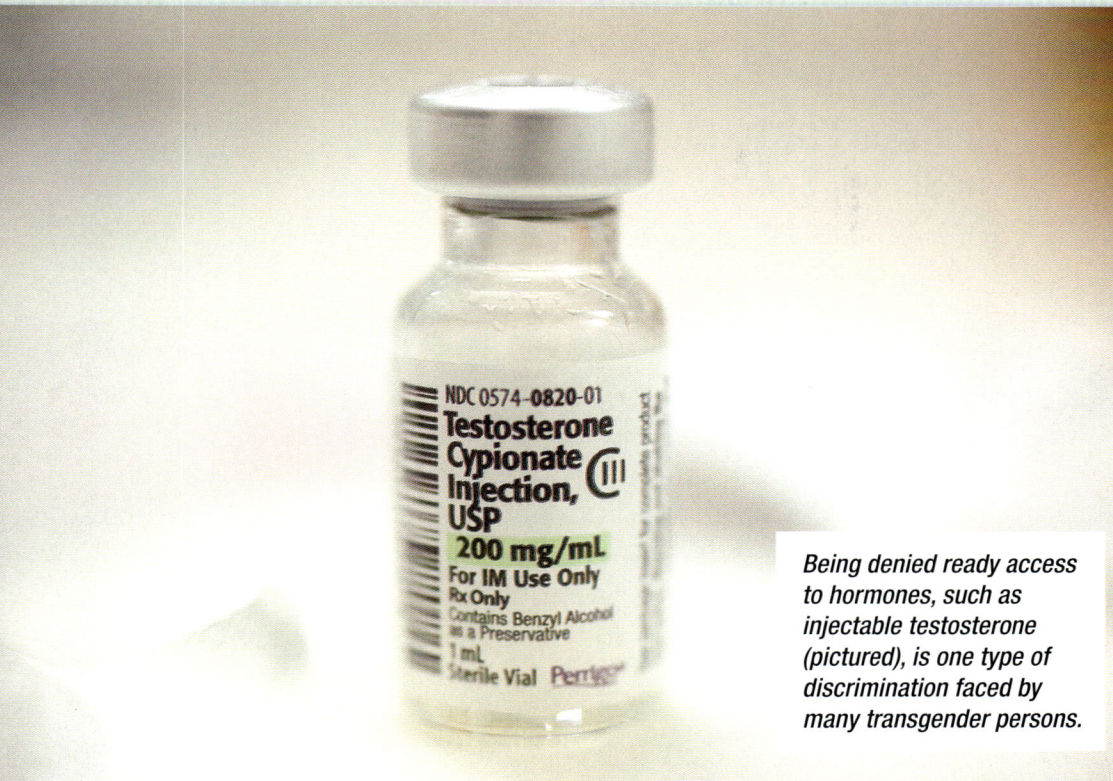

Being denied ready access to hormones, such as injectable testosterone (pictured), is one type of discrimination faced by many transgender persons.

In addition, Mark states, he has suffered from discrimination in other ways and sees those negative experiences as "a microcosm [small-scale example] of the much bigger problem. By that, I mean the widespread ignorance, fear, and hatred of LGBTQ people that has long plagued society." These unpleasant realities, he suggests, have led to discrimination "not only in the area of health care but in lots of other social areas as well."9

The Center, the Human Rights Campaign (HRC), the American Civil Liberties Union (ACLU), and other organizations that advocate for equal rights for all citizens agree on one point: anti-LGBTQ discrimination exists in numerous areas of American society. These include workplaces across the country, where employees have long felt reluctant to reveal they are gay or trans for fear of being fired. There has also been much opposition to LGBTQ people serving in the military, including a ban instituted by President Donald J. Trump in 2017. (The ban was reversed by President Joseph R. Biden early in 2021.)

"Widespread ignorance, fear, and hatred of LGBTQ people . . . has long plagued society."9

—Mark, a trans man

Bans on LGBTQ Students Participating in School Sports

Another frequent area of anti-LGBTQ discrimination, say equal rights advocates, is school sports. Some school systems and states have long feared allowing LGBTQ students, particularly transgender ones, on sports teams. Among the reasons given for this attitude is that allowing them to compete would be somehow disruptive of or detrimental to the team and the school.

One of many attempts by state legislatures to prohibit trans and other LGBTQ athletes from playing occurred in South Dakota in 2021. House Bill 1217 was designed to keep female trans students from competing on teams matching their gender identity. Trans students who originally had male bodies but female gender

The Effects of Remote Learning on LGBTQ Youth

Several problems that young LGBTQ people typically face in high school were amplified during the COVID-19 pandemic. To keep the virus from spreading, most schools across the country switched to remote learning on home computers. Pulitzer Prize–nominated journalist Bianca Quilantan explains some of the negative effects this had on LGBTQ students:

> [Having] been thrown onto the Zoom-sphere due to the pandemic, some of them are grappling with having to reel back their gender identity and exploration while at home because they're not out to their parents. . . . Students are also unable to linger after class to develop relationships with teachers who often become some of their greatest advocates. These students, who are at a higher risk for poor mental health and suicide [than] their peers, are as a result especially struggling to find affirmation. While research is being conducted on the pandemic's effect on LGBTQ youth . . . suicide prevention nonprofit The Trevor Project said the number of people accessing its crisis support has significantly increased. . . . Being disconnected from in-person supports could mean additional hurdles for students who are already fragile.

Bianca Quilantan, "Pandemic Collides with Concerns About LGBTQ Students' Mental Health," Politico, December 14, 2020. www.politico.com.

---

identities wanted to play on girls' teams. Those opposed argued that they were not really "girls," so they should not be allowed to compete on all-girl teams.

This was the seventh attempt by a group of South Dakota lawmakers to keep trans students off school sports teams. Like the others, it failed to pass. But the margin between passage and nonpassage was slim, say those who oppose laws of that sort. Moreover, many such bills continue to be proposed across the nation. Ella Schneiberg of the HRC comments that "there is a coordinated attack on trans kids being waged in state legislatures across the country right now. And one of the most common bills that we're tracking targets trans athletes."[10] Schneiberg based that statement on the fact that in February 2021, twenty-two such anti-trans legislative bills were under consideration in seventeen US states.

Lingering Social Stigma

Physicians, psychologists, and other experts who specialize in LGBTQ issues pinpoint where the recurring urge to discriminate against gay and trans people, including younger ones, comes from. It stems, they say, from feelings, beliefs, and fears buried deeply in society's underlying fabric. As a result of these ideas and fears, the experts explain, trans and other LGBTQ students have acquired a social stigma—a sort of badge of shame or dishonor. This stigma is based on their nonconformity with the sexual norms of society's heterosexual majority. Many straight people do not understand or trust the differences between straight and LGBTQ people. For many, religion has perpetuated this distrust, but other social institutions, including legal systems and media, have reinforced it. Hence, historically straight society has tended to react to LGBTQ individuals with suspicion, fear, hostility, and discrimination.

This lingering social stigma, the experts contend, has had various hurtful and detrimental effects on members of the LGBTQ community. In the words of Weill Cornell Medical College scholar and physician Dhruv Khullar,

> For decades, we've known that lesbian, gay, bisexual and transgender individuals experience a range of social, economic, and health disparities, often the result of a culture and of laws and policies that treat them as lesser human beings. They're more likely to struggle with poverty and social isolation. They have a higher risk of mental health problems, substance use, and smoking. Sexual minorities live, on average, shorter lives than heterosexuals, and LGBT youth are three times as likely to contemplate suicide, and nearly five times as likely to *attempt* suicide.[11]

From Homophobia to an Explicit Denial of Rights

The social, economic, and health disparities and unfair treatment that Khullar mentions take several forms. For students in particular, social exclusion is one form. It often consists of trying to keep LGBTQ people off school sports teams and out of clubs, dance committees, and other common social activities. Other frequent types of mistreatment of LGBTQ individuals include name-calling, harassment, and other types of overt homophobia.

In addition to these basic forms of anti-LGBTQ discrimination are those that involve an explicit denial of rights. They have in the past included, and in some areas still include, banning same-sex marriage; denying someone federal benefits; discrimination in employment, including firing someone for being gay or trans; and refusing to give someone health care benefits.

All of these can have serious health consequences, either physical or mental, Khullar and other experts point out. They emphasize that the connection between social stigma and adverse physical and psychological effects on LGBTQ people has been repeatedly proven by studies and statistics. For example, Khullar

A gay couple dances at their wedding. Studies have shown that in states that have legalized same-sex marriage, the move has had a positive effect on the mental health and well-being of young LGBTQ people.

states, it has been documented that "sexual minorities living in communities with high levels of prejudice die more than a decade earlier than those in less prejudiced communities."[12] Also, almost 10 percent of gay and lesbian people, and at least 30 percent of trans people, report having been refused needed health care treatment because of their sexual orientation or gender identity, as happened to Mark in Iowa.

Furthermore, the experts say, the ill effects caused by lingering social stigma disproportionately affect LGBTQ individuals who are in their teens and twenties. This has been proven by recent studies of the effects on young people's health and well-being when states expand the rights of LGBTQ youth or, conversely, restrict them. For instance, following Massachusetts's legalization of same-sex marriage in 2003, Khullar recalls, "mental health visits

She Only Wanted to Go to the Bathroom

Mark, a transgender man who experienced prejudice at the hands of doctors in Iowa in 2016, is one of many individuals who has felt put upon by ingrained social fears of trans people. He was already an adult at the time, but many of the trans individuals who have suffered from discrimination have been teenagers still in school. Among their number is Esmée Silverman, who attended high school in Easton, Massachusetts. She remembers how she felt when, in 2017, President Donald J. Trump canceled existing protections on trans people using public bathrooms:

> I was going through this horrible depressive episode. I was living in constant fear that I was going to be judged because of my identity. And when I finally came out at the end of freshman year and saw [Trump's directive rescinding protections for transgender students], I was like, *Are you kidding me?* If you got to know me, you'll know I don't want to hurt anyone. And the fact that some Republicans were saying this was because [trans] people are trying to go into bathrooms to stalk people—it hurts me. We just want to go to the bathroom. I remember feeling anxious and depressed about it.

Quoted in Molly Olmstead, "What This Moment Feels Like for the Victims of Trump's Cruelest Policies," *Slate*, November 10, 2020. https://slate.com.

dropped significantly for gay men across the state. Other states that followed suit saw a 7 percent reduction in suicide attempts among LGBT adolescents. Nationwide, legalization of same-sex marriage is linked to increases in the likelihood that gay men have health insurance and a regular doctor to see." He adds, however, that "by contrast, in states that passed same-sex marriage bans in 2004 and 2006, LGBT individuals experienced a marked rise in mental health problems, including anxiety, alcohol use, and mood disorders. (No such increase was found in neighboring states that did not pass bans.)"[13]

How Ignorance Can Lead to Discrimination

The experts say that homophobia has no single root cause but that those who do discriminate tend to be ignorant of what it actually means to be lesbian, gay, bi, or trans. Former US attorney general Loretta Lynch, who has dealt with several cases of anti-LGBTQ discrimination, has stated, "So much of what we see in terms of hate crimes or bullying or bias [against LGBTQ individuals] stems from ignorance. It stems from fear. It stems from labeling someone else as different, labeling someone else as 'other,' not realizing that we're all different."[14]

Lynch and other people familiar with the evidence say that such ignorance regularly takes the form of believing age-old myths about LGBTQ people, not realizing they are either stereotypes or simply false. Typical is the mistaken notion that a gay or trans person chooses to be that way. The truth, medical and other experts say, is that LGBTQ individuals are born that way.

> "So much of what we see in terms of hate crimes or bullying [against LGBTQ people] stems from ignorance."[14]
>
> —Loretta Lynch, the former US attorney general

What is more, Lynch has pointed out, people who distrust, dislike, or discriminate against LGBTQ individuals are usually unaware of the damage they do. In most cases, they do not understand how much pain and suffering they inflict. Some of that damage is to the nation itself, she says, because it works to deprive people of their full civil rights. "This is a great country, as you know," Lynch asserts. "But it's only great if everyone has a chance to participate and everyone has a chance to be seen for who they truly are."[15]

Homophobia Is Still Common

The more visible and tangible harm caused by anti-LGBTQ discrimination, Lynch and other experts explain, impacts human beings. In schools, for instance, it can lead to bullying, various types of humiliation, making it hard for the victims to learn, and even out-and-out physical violence. In 2020 the noted LGBTQ education advocacy group GLSEN (formerly the Gay, Lesbian, and Straight Education Network) announced the results of a major study in which it surveyed students in all fifty states as well as the District of Columbia and the US territories of Puerto Rico, American Samoa, and Guam. The study revealed that homophobia is still common in the vast majority of US schools.

For example, GLSEN's interviewers found that a colossal 97 percent of LGBTQ students between the ages of thirteen and twenty-one had experienced negative and mean-spirited comments about their sexual orientation or gender identity. Also, roughly 69 percent said they had been verbally harassed. Another 57 percent of the nation's LGBTQ students reported being threatened with bodily harm at least once by fellow students. Backing up these figures were the results of a study published in the *American Journal of Preventive Medicine* in 2020. It found that 91 percent of LGBTQ teenagers in the United States had been bullied for being gay or trans at least once, either inside or outside of school.

Such bullying does not typically include physical assault, although the studies show that at times it does. "In some of the most disturbing news [that came out of GLSEN's survey]," reports noted pop culture commentator Mey Rude, a quarter of the students surveyed stated that they "have been physically harassed. Eleven percent have been assaulted at school because of their gender or orientation." As a result of these attacks, Rude

The bullying and mistreatment that most LGBTQ youths face in school can leave them feeling lonely and depressed.

goes on, "nearly a third of LGBTQ+ students said they have even skipped an entire day of school in the previous month because they feared for their safety."[16]

The Consequences of Discrimination

In addition, various surveys demonstrate that such discrimination and mistreatment frequently do considerable harm to LGBTQ students' sense of self-worth and ability to learn. The periodic missing of school to avoid harassment, for instance, sometimes "leads to lower GPAs [grade point averages] and a decreased desire to pursue post-secondary education," states the Center for American Progress. Moreover, the center states, "lesbian, gay, and bisexual youth are roughly four times more likely to consider or attempt suicide than their straight peers. Similarly, transgender students are approximately four to six times more likely to attempt suicide than their cisgender [nontrans] peers."[17]

Even if the outcome is not fatal, it is not uncommon for bullying and mistreatment to fill a young person's years as a student—from elementary school through high school—with uncertainty and misery. Athena Schwartz, who attended school in Utah, is one of numerous young people who have found themselves in such an unfortunate situation. She recalls,

> For most of my elementary school years, people always hung out with their gendered groups. I often found myself alone, and when I would try to fit in with others I would be made fun of. I remember for my seventh birthday, some girl gave me a "Thomas the Train" toy and told me she got that for me because that's what boys like. I cried and cried to my mom because I wasn't a boy. I had always known that I wasn't a girl either, but I didn't know what I was until high school. Even when I came out as nonbinary, I still faced being bullied for not being "normal." I've never fit in the norm and I'm still working on fully understanding that it's OK.[18]

Another young LGBTQ person whose life was negatively influenced by discrimination was Tae Johnson, who now attends Prairie View A&M University in Texas. She recalls with much regret, "I first experienced bullying when I was in elementary school, but the most extreme point was when I reached middle school. I used to get verbally and physically harassed every day to the point I hated waking up in the morning and I seriously battled with finding the strength to continue living."[19]

Stories like these, along with the general detrimental effects of anti-LGBTQ prejudice in society at large, are what have inspired numerous people in their teens and twenties to become activists for LGBTQ causes. Johnson herself, for example, eventually overcame the emotional trauma she underwent in school by channeling her energies into positive thought and action. "I knew at a young age," she states, that "if I made it through that point of my life I'd be able to help kids like myself in the future."[20] Now she helps younger LGBTQ students deal with some of the same negative issues she personally experienced.

CHAPTER TWO

The Activists

"[I was] afraid to be growing up in this world where I'm not wanted and not accepted," recalls Aryn Bucci-Mooney, a high school senior in Albany, New York. He remembers his feelings of insecurity at age twelve at the beginning of Donald J. Trump's presidency. After joining the boys' soccer team, Aryn was bullied and made fun of because he had recently come out as transgender. Aryn says Trump's ideas and policies validated "the idea that we are not human beings, that it's OK to discriminate against us simply because we were born in the wrong body; that it's OK to take away a student's right to feel safe."[21] The mistreatment got so bad, the young man says, that he eventually quit the team.

In the months and years that followed, however, Aryn underwent a profound, positive transformation. He decided he was not going to take any more abuse and rapidly channeled his anger and youthful energies into activism, not only for himself but also on behalf of other young LGBTQ people. In school, he joined the wrestling team, where he made a real name for himself. He also joined local school and regional groups working to eliminate anti-LGBTQ discrimination in upstate New York. These activities included helping to train teachers in how to be sensitive to the needs of gay and trans students. His efforts stood out so much that the national organization GLSEN chose him as a member of its elite group of young LGBTQ activists—the GLSEN National Student Council—for the 2020–2021 season. Despite receiving this and other honors, Aryn remains both humble and focused on those who need aid and comfort, as he once did. "It makes such an extraordinary difference to kids when they aren't feeling confident in themselves, to have and know that somebody is there looking out for them,"[22] he states.

From Fictional Character to National Organization

Aryn found that the national exposure he received through working with GLSEN allowed him to reach and help many more young people than he could have without that major recognition. In fact, all LGBTQ activists—young and old—agree that although the efforts of individual activists are vital, by themselves they are not enough. To effect large-scale change, such individuals need to band together into countrywide organizations that can exert considerable social and political clout. This is how GLSEN and other national pro-LGBTQ groups came to be.

Among those organizations, one of the most famous and successful is the Trevor Project. It was established in 1998 by the makers of the Oscar-winning short film *Trevor*. Back in 1994, producers Peggy Rajski and Randy Stone decided to shoot a film bringing to life the character Trevor, whom writer Celeste Lecesne had earlier created to illustrate the struggles that many young trans individuals go through. Lecesne penned the screenplay and Rajski directed the film, which went on to receive international praise and various awards.

Indeed, the portrayal of Trevor in the film touched and inspired large numbers of people of all walks of life, including prominent members of the LGBTQ community. The film's producers received numerous requests to somehow use the project as a basis for a real-life organization that could help struggling trans and other LGBTQ young people. Following these requests, Rajski contacted several widely respected mental health experts. They helped her to put together the logistical resources required to create a nationwide twenty-four-hour crisis hotline. Today, that

In 1998 the producers of the Oscar-winning film Trevor, Peggy Rajski and Randy Stone, formed a national organization called the Trevor Project to advocate on behalf of LGBTQ young people.

group, which the founders named the Trevor Project, is widely recognized as the leading national organization devoted to delivering crisis intervention and suicide prevention services to LGBTQ people under age twenty-five.

Goals, Strategy, and Services

One reason why Rajski moved forward with the Trevor Project in 1998 is because the experts she consulted told her that a national LGBTQ organization with a hotline was desperately needed. Suicide rates among trans and other LGBTQ youth were extremely high, they pointed out. Even today, although lower than in the past, those rates remain frighteningly high. According to Trevor Project officials,

> LGBTQ young people are more than four times more likely to attempt suicide than their peers, and suicide remains the second leading cause of death among all young people in the United States. In 2019, our research team published the nation's first estimate of LGBTQ youth considering suicide in partnership with leading experts from across the country. This ground-breaking research showed that over 1.8 million LGBTQ young people in the United States consider suicide each year.[23]

The Trevor Project's primary goal is to reduce the high incidence of suicidal thoughts and actions among young LGBTQ people. The group's chief strategy in accomplishing that aim has been to coordinate a team of hundreds of dedicated volunteers across the country. Many of these individuals operate the hotline, called the Trevor Lifeline, which is open twenty-four hours a day, every day of the year. An online version is also available for those young people who prefer not to use their phones to make contact.

> "Over 1.8 million LGBTQ young people in the United States consider suicide each year."[23]
>
> —The Trevor Project

The organization offers a wide range of services to help struggling LGBTQ youth in addition to its phone and online hotlines. One of these services, TrevorSpace, consists of a social networking community for LGBTQ youth between the ages of thirteen and twenty-four. Friends and allies of those individuals are also welcomed into friendly discussions in which LGBTQ young people share their personal stories, talk about their feelings, and discuss a wide range of social and political issues. This safe social space for young people is used by tens of thousands of people daily. Rep-

Advanced Technology to Help Reduce Suicides

Most of the national pro-LGBTQ organizations use the latest technological advances to make it easier and more efficient to help at-risk young people. Here, Kendra Gaunt, a young activist at the Trevor Project, explains how the group recently installed cutting edge computers with artificial intelligence (AI) capabilities.

> With the support of $2.7 million in Google.org grant funding . . . we have introduced new AI applications to scale [up] our impact. We built an AI system that helps us identify which LGBTQ individuals reaching out to us for support are at the highest risk of suicide so that we can quickly connect them to counselors who are ready to help at that moment. I joined The Trevor Project because it's an organization driven by values, and our use of technology reflects this. I noticed an opportunity to leverage my years of experience and partner with people who are committed to employing technology for social good. Through the thoughtful and ethical use of AI, we can overcome obstacles of scale and complexity as we pursue our mission to end suicide among LGBTQ youth.

Kendra Gaunt, "How the Trevor Project Continues to Support LGBTQ Youth," *The Keyword* (blog), Google, September 30, 2020. https://blog.google.

resented are contributors from every US state and more than one hundred other nations.

Another service the organization offers—known as TrevorChat—is aimed at young LGBTQ people who feel the need to talk about their feelings and problems with a trained counselor. To that end, professional therapists who regularly volunteer their time are available every day of the year. Of the many other services that the Trevor Project offers, one of the most progressive and effective is the Trevor Youth Advisory Council. Similar to GLSEN's National Student Council, it consists of twenty young activists, ages sixteen to twenty-four, chosen each year from states around the country. These young advocates raise awareness in their communities about mental health issues concerning LGBTQ youth. In addition, the Trevor Project publishes and widely distributes *Coming Out: A Handbook for LGBTQ Young People*, which discusses gender, orientation, social relationships, dating, and other relevant issues.

An Enormous Impact on the Media

The positive impact of the Trevor Project has been substantial. In surveys of young LGBTQ people who used the Trevor Lifeline, a majority of those in states of crisis said they had experienced a major reduction in their levels of desperation after talking to Trevor volunteers.

Many members of the LGBTQ community, young and old alike, have experienced similar levels of relief in various ways from their interactions with another pro-LGBTQ organization. Its full name was originally the Gay & Lesbian Alliance Against Defamation, but it announced in 2013 that it would thereafter be called only by its acronym: GLAAD.

The group was established in 1985 as a means of protesting against what its founders perceived as defamatory, or offensive, coverage of LGBTQ people in both national and local media. At the time, for instance, newspapers, magazines, and television news broadcasts carried numerous stories about victims of acquired immunodeficiency syndrome (AIDS). A large percentage of those patients were gay, and most of the media reports tended to use homophobic or other insulting words and phrases. GLAAD's

Members of the Trevor Project march in the 2013 Gay Pride Parade in New York City. The Trevor Project offers a wide range of services to help struggling LGBTQ youth.

initial goal was to educate journalists and other media writers and producers in how to talk about LGBTQ people in neutral, inoffensive ways.

Over time, the group added to its agenda the role of watchdog over the entire entertainment industry, specifically in how that business portrays LGBTQ people, both real and fictional. Today, GLAAD regularly and closely monitors film, television, music, and other media to make sure that those portrayals are accurate, fair, and do not insult or defame gay and trans individuals. In addition, trained members of GLAAD's staff work directly with film and television executives, producers, directors, and writers; often those GLAAD staffers see scripts in advance and give advice on how to make LGBTQ story lines and characters as realistic and fair as possible.

GLAAD also works hard to help LGBTQ people around the globe gain acceptance and fair media treatment in their respective countries. One typical approach is to advise local pro-LGBTQ groups in those nations on how to best achieve their goals. A striking example of success in that regard occurred in 2015, when GLAAD helped Irish LGBTQ activists win marriage equality in that country. (Ireland was the first nation to make same-sex marriage legal in a countrywide referendum.)

GLAAD's impact on the film and television industries, as well as on social acceptance of LGBTQ people worldwide, has been enormous. As GLAAD's president and chief executive officer, Sarah Kate Ellis, puts it,

> In the past decade, we've really seen the tables turn from being a watchdog to a partner to Hollywood. . . . One of the significant things is that Hollywood, like the rest of the revenue-driven America, understands that diversity and inclusion matter deeply, and that if people aren't represented [fairly in the media] they won't pay to come see stories [created by the media].[24]

Among the other leading progressive organizations that aid and support members of the LGBTQ community is the ACLU. Founded during the 1920s, the ACLU's mission is to defend the rights guaranteed in the US Constitution to all Americans, including LGBTQ people. ACLU attorneys often sue in court to try to uphold such rights. A recent example was a suit the organization filed in 2020 on behalf of six trans members of the US armed forces; the suit contended that the Trump administration's ban on trans people serving in the US military was a form of discrimination.

Ezra's Speeches on Gender Identity

Some of the other prominent organizations that support LGBTQ rights and needs include the Center, the HRC, the Transgender Law Center, and the Matthew Shepard Foundation. These and still other pro-LGBTQ groups regularly influence, inspire, consult, work with, or even sometimes hire individual LGBTQ activists. In each passing year, a large proportion of those activists who are new to this sort of work tend to be on the young side—in their teens and early twenties.

Typical of these earnest, hardworking young individuals is Texas high school student Ezra Morales, whose advocacy work for various LGBTQ causes has been impressive. He first became active in that area during his freshman year in high school. Ezra worked closely with representatives of GLSEN who were trying to improve treatment of LGBTQ students in the region. Later, he worked with the HRC on both the local and national level. In his school, as well as at conferences held in Texas and other states, he wrote and delivered public speeches and led workshops attended by people of all ages.

In his speeches, Ezra specializes in reporting what his research has revealed about the realities of gender identity. That subject is far more complex and misunderstood than most people realize, he points out. He explains that in the simplest sense he is a boy. However, he says, "my gender expression doesn't align with tra-

Success for a Young Native American Activist

Henry Roanhorse Gray is a Native American LGBTQ activist from Tulsa, Oklahoma. He is one of the cofounders of the group Osage Citizens for Marriage Equality. While in his late teens and early twenties, Gray played a key role in the successful battle to make same-sex marriage legal in the Osage Nation, one of the country's biggest Native American tribes. Gray wrote articles, made speeches, and spoke in person with people to convince other members of the tribe to vote yes on same-sex marriage. That, he said, would be the fairest, most humane choice. When the referendum took place in 2017, more than half of the Osage who turned out to vote agreed with him, and the measure passed. Although the US Supreme Court made same-sex marriage legal in 2015, that decision did not affect Native American reservations, which, legally speaking, are sovereign nations. Hence, each tribe decides for itself whether to allow same-sex marriage. For example, the Cherokee Nation and the Cheyenne and Arapaho tribes legalized same-sex marriage before 2017. Gray says he hopes that other Native American nations will do the same.

ditional gender norms for boys." He continues, "No matter how hard I try to fit into the label of 'boy' or 'girl,' I will never be afforded the same status as [most boys] of that gender."[25]

Miguel in Missouri; Rowan in Kentucky

Another accomplished young activist, Miguel Johnson from St. Joseph, Missouri, graduated from high school in 2020. Chosen as a member of GLSEN's prestigious National Student Council early in his school career, he felt the urge to speak out against a ban that prohibited trans students from using regular school bathrooms. Feeling he was a target of blatant discrimination, he blamed President Trump, who had recently encouraged and backed such bans around the country. "Before Trump got elected," Miguel told an interviewer for *People* magazine, "he always said he was totally for LGBTQ students." But later, "after he got elected, he was basically like, 'Just kidding, I lied.'"[26]

In 2017 Miguel was invited to cohost that year's GLSEN Respect Awards ceremony. His fellow awards presenter was none

The Gay & Lesbian Alliance Against Defamation (GLAAD) works with Hollywood's executives, producers, directors, and writers to make certain that portrayals of LGBTQ individuals are fair and accurate.

other than Oscar-winning actor Julia Roberts, the event's featured guest. The two talked at length, and Roberts was duly impressed. She later told *People*,

> I had the pleasure of presenting, [along] with Miguel, [the] GLSEN Respect Awards, and Miguel, like all the students I met there, is smart, kind, and incredibly brave to live their life openly and honestly at such a young age. As a parent, I want all students to feel safe and protected at school, and I stand with Miguel and trans students across the country.[27]

Another young LGBTQ activist, Rowan Little, who is a year younger than Miguel, went to a Kentucky high school known to be more progressive than most schools in that state. As Rowan explains, "One thing that made our school stand out from the rest is the rapid growth in support of its LGBTQ students, made possible by several important changes by the administration."[28] It was especially important to Rowan that he and his classmates be treated with respect and kindness. He identifies as gender fluid; gender fluid people feel that their gender is not always fixed, but that it can and does change over time. "Some days I feel like my gender could be like what I was assigned at birth," he explains. "But there are some days when I feel the opposite way."[29]

The school's administrators made it clear to the student body, Rowan says, that unconventional gender identities such as his would always be respected. Also, the principal promised, the school would be a safe space for LGBTQ students. In fact, Rowan himself played a role in the ongoing process of creating a friendly school atmosphere. He recalls that one day

> "As a parent, I want all students to feel safe and protected at school."[27]
>
> —Julia Roberts, an Oscar-winning actor

> my principal invited me to his office to discuss how things could be improved for LGBTQ students. . . . I had several ideas. For instance, I told him that our two gender-neutral bathrooms were very hard for some students to access during the school day, because our school has three separate buildings. He responded by making plans to open another gender-neutral bathroom in one of the annexes.[30]

Rowan adds, "I am so proud of my school and of the positive school climate they have fostered, and I'm excited for all the opportunities [the students] have to further learn and expand in the future."[31] It is his heartfelt hope that in that future the schools of all LGBTQ youth will be that way. In such a world, after all, there will be far less need for LGBTQ activists because there will be far less discrimination.

CHAPTER THREE

The Teen Activist's Tool Kit

In 2018, when he was a high school sophomore in Orange County, California, Jaiden Blancaflor felt overcome by emotional distress. As a young trans person, he later recalled, "I didn't like how I was living my life. I wanted more interaction with the LGBTQ community." The problem, Jaiden says, was that he felt alone much of the time, in large part because "all my friends were cis [straight] people."[32]

Fortunately for Jaiden, he was aware of the existence of the hotline at the Trevor Project, and without hesitation he dialed the number. The person who answered, he remembers, understood the situation and calmly, patiently talked about Jaiden's personal feelings at that moment, as well as how he felt about his life in general. "After we talked," Jaiden later explained, "I felt more understood, more valid."[33]

Jaiden felt so much better after the call that he was inspired to become openly active in LGBTQ causes and groups at school. "I started writing down . . . ways I could relieve some of the stress I was feeling about schoolwork," he says. "I decided I should start planning Pride Week"[34] with other LGBTQ students. The more involved Jaiden became in such activities, the more he realized that being connected to members of the LGBTQ community was a crucial way to feel better about himself. Moreover, the most obvious way to connect with other young LGBTQ students was through social media of various kinds. After all, he reasoned, in the modern world, social media platforms often constitute the fastest way to reach large numbers of people. As a fledgling activist, Jaiden decided not only to use social media to improve his own situation but also "to create ways for [LGBTQ] people to connect with others [like themselves] in the community."[35]

Mental health experts agree wholeheartedly with Jaiden's gut instincts in this case. Molly Longman, a reporter on health issues for *Teen Vogue* and other magazines, says social support from one's peers can be a major factor in young people's maintenance of normal, strong mental health. Longman points out that a survey in the prestigious *Journal of Counseling Psychology* shows that "while experiences of prejudice and fear of anti-trans stigma are associated with a higher risk of depression and suicide, those who reported having greater social support had a lower risk of these [negative] outcomes."[36]

More Involvement in School and the Community

Another successful way for LGBTQ youth to feel respected, healthy, and happy is to form and maintain school-based GSAs. Those letters sometimes stand for "Gay-Straight Alliance." In other instances—in Jaiden's school, for example—they delineate "Gender and Sexuality Alliance." Whatever the participants choose to call them, these groups are essentially local clubs whose members share ideas, plan social events, and work to create positive images of the LGBTQ community.

Suraj Singareddy, a gay Indian American student at Northview High School in Johns Creek, Georgia, was elected president of his school's GSA. One of the leading teen LGBTQ activists in the country, Suraj was also chosen as a member of GLSEN's 2020–2021 National Student Council. About his GSA, he says, "I think it's really helped people just find that support network that they might be missing elsewhere." He adds, "We're just trying to become a larger part of the Northview community because in the past, we've kind of been low on everyone's priority list. We're

One way for LGBTQ youth to feel respected, healthy, and happy is to form clubs in which they collaborate with straight students to share ideas, plan events, and work to create positive images of the LGBTQ community.

really trying to change up [the] GSA to make it more involved in the school."[37]

Hoping to inspire that increased involvement, Suraj instituted a hefty list of activities, some designed to foster cooperation among the GSA's members and others to give the school's LGBTQ students stronger ties to the greater community. For example, he points out, "we are definitely doing a lot more volunteering. We did phone banking back in June, [and] we are planning to organize a workshop for teachers so that they can learn how to better advocate for their [LGBTQ] students."[38] Suraj, along with the GSA's secretary, Maansi Manoj, also led the members in a fund-raiser for an Atlanta-based group that supports trans and gay women. "I'm looking forward to some of the topics and discussions we have going on later in the year," states Maansi, about societal topics "like Medicaid expansion [and] how that affects healthcare [for members of] the LGBTQ community."[39]

Another member of GLSEN's 2020–2021 National Student Council, Eric Samelo, also helped to create a GSA at his high school. A student at Loveless Academy Magnet Program High School in Montgomery, Alabama, in 2019 Eric received a distinct local honor: he accepted the Stephen Light Youth Activism Award in a public ceremony attended by the town's police chief and other dignitaries.

In accepting the award, Eric recalled why he and a classmate had formed the GSA a year before. Sometimes various students had given the two friends judgmental looks or muttered remarks under their breath, he said. The two boys reacted by starting the LGBTQ club, and not long afterward they learned of its positive impact. A female member of the group told them that the GSA was the only place outside her home where she felt completely safe. Eric concluded his speech at the ceremony by saying, with a touch of emotion in his voice, "I just want to make sure that they feel loved and safe and welcomed because everyone deserves that."[40]

> "I just want to make sure that they feel loved and safe and welcomed because everyone deserves that."[40]
>
> —Eric Samelo, an activist in Alabama

Taking One's Grievance to Court

Some LGBTQ students have brought about positive change in their schools by using more direct—or, at times, more confrontational—methods than influencing people's opinions through social media or school clubs. The more direct approach has been to lobby one's school administration, asking the principal or other officials to initiate various LGBTQ-friendly changes. This was the approach that Rowan Little had employed with his school administration. In that case, the effort was successful, as the principal was receptive to instituting fair, constructive changes.

Other LGBTQ students have opted for the more confrontational, combative route of taking their grievances at school to court. Perhaps the most celebrated case of that type in recent years was that of Drew Adams, whose 2020 court victory made national headlines. Covered less often in the national media yet still important, however, have been dozens of other similar cases brought by young LGBTQ people who felt their basic rights as citizens had been denied.

One of those young court litigants was Gavin Grimm, who graduated from a Virginia high school in 2017. When he entered the school, his mother explained to the school's administrators that he was undergoing emotional difficulties related to his male transgender identity and needed to use the boys' bathrooms at school. Permission was initially granted, but after a few months the school reversed itself and banned the young man from the boys' facilities.

The Grimm family contacted the ACLU, which took the case to court. A Virginia judge ruled in Grimm's favor in 2019, but the school system appealed the case to the Fourth Circuit Court of Appeals in Washington, DC. In 2020, the judges also handed Grimm a victory, saying, "We have little difficulty holding that a bathroom policy precluding Grimm from using the boys restrooms discriminated against him on the basis of sex."[41]

From Bullied Child to LGBTQ Champion

Although some LGBTQ students have managed to effect changes in school policies by speaking to school administrators or going to court, a few of these young activists have taken an even more daring route: they have gone right to their state legislatures. With the backing of sympathetic parents and pro–civil rights groups like the ACLU, they have forcefully urged lawmakers to either institute LGBTQ-friendly legislation or alter older laws.

An outstanding example of this method of securing LGBTQ rights is the case of New Jersey student activist Rebekah Bruesehoff. She turned fourteen in January 2021, but her fame stems from what she did in the preceding two years, beginning when she was only twelve. In a series of moves that have amazed and inspired millions of people—LGBTQ and non-LGBTQ alike—she publicly lobbied the New Jersey state legislature and convinced

Easing the Fight for Equal Treatment

Not all LGBTQ high school students have experienced struggles or confrontations with their school administrations. An inspiring example of LGBTQ students working together with their school principal occurred in 2020–2021 in a small high school in Lowell, Massachusetts. There, the principal, Chuck Puga, heard that one of the incoming students, Ashton Mota, was transgender. Puga's reaction was to reach out and be kind and welcoming. Young Ashton recalls,

> When I started high school, I was nervous because I didn't know what to expect. Knowing that I was transgender, my school administrator proactively sought me out during the first week of school to casually check in with me and see how I was adjusting to school life. The administrator told me that my only job and goal at school was to be a student, and that I didn't have to take on the weight of educating faculty and staff about trans inclusion. . . . Needless to say, his response made me feel safe and comfortable . . . [and] more connected to my school, which has helped me to thrive.

Puga himself says, "We are continually working on building a school culture of respect and dignity for all students."

Ashton Mota, "Leading by Example: How School Principals Can Support LGBTQ Students," Human Rights Campaign, September 22, 2020. www.hrc.org.

---

those lawmakers to create a law that will positively affect that state's LGBTQ school students for years to come.

The story of "Mighty Rebekah," as many people have come to call her, began when she was six and started attending public school. Because she was trans—a girl trapped in a boy's body, of which she and her parents were already aware—she was bullied frequently and cruelly. Eventually she had to change schools because many of her classmates' parents thought she would be a bad influence on other children. Her mother, Jamie Bruesehoff, later described the anguish the child and her family endured. "It's hard to be different from everyone else and not be accepted," Bruesehoff remarked. "No one prepares you for a 7½-year-old who wants to die."[42]

Transgender student activist Rebekah Bruesehoff publicly lobbied New Jersey's legislature to create a law that requires the state's schools to teach facts about LGBTQ individuals in their courses on the historical contributions of LGBTQ people.

After a while, Rebekah went through a gender transition in which she dressed as and pursued the normal activities of a girl. Following that, her parents say, she underwent a rapid and powerful shift in attitude. No longer depressed and afraid, she embraced her identity and professed a desire to help other LGBTQ children and teens. "I was heartbroken," she said, that they were bullied, and "I decided I [needed] to keep speaking for the people who need the message of hope and acceptance." She wanted to become their champion, she said. "It's what I was meant to do."[43]

Showdown in Trenton

Rebekah thought long and hard about the different ways she could be an LGBTQ activist and discussed it with her parents and other trusted adults. In time, she decided that the most far-reaching and long-lasting change would result from advocating for the passage of new pro-LGBTQ laws. In particular, it bothered her that schools in her state did not include any facts about LGBTQ history in their courses; and she reasoned that one reason why so much anti-LGBTQ prejudice existed was because few people knew what gay and trans people had gone through over the centuries. Her idea was that by including a bit of LGBTQ history in school curricula, people like herself would seem less different and scary to straight people.

> "I decided I [needed] to keep speaking for the people who need the message of hope and acceptance."[43]
>
> —Rebekah Bruesehoff, an activist in New Jersey

With that goal in mind, in December 2018 twelve-year-old Rebekah stunned both onlookers and the press by testifying before New Jersey's legislature in the state capital of Trenton. In her showdown with adult lawmakers, she explained her well-thought-out ideas for a new law that would mandate teaching about the abuses LGBTQ people had long endured as a result of hatred and bigotry. "I was really nervous," the teen later remembered. "I knew these people had a lot of power, and I didn't know how they were going to respond to me being me. But I was excited for the [legislative] bill so kids like me could learn about other kids like us."[44]

Many people across the state and beyond were astonished once more when a mere two months later the legislature passed the new law Rebekah had fought for. The bill states, in part, that New Jersey boards of education must "include instruction, and adopt instructional materials, that accurately portray political, economic, and social contributions of persons with disabilities and lesbian, gay, bisexual, and transgender people."[45] The new law went into effect during the 2020–2021 school year.

Thereafter, the gutsy teen became newsworthy not only for what she had accomplished in the political and legal sphere. Numerous people will never forget what she has said on several occasions since then about her experiences of being both trans and an LGBTQ activist. These things, she stated, "inspired me

A Deal Too Sweet To Resist

"The hero stands in a resolute pose," journalist John Potter writes, "her bright hair swirling around her face. She calls her team to action as a flag flaps in the wind behind her. It's the stuff of comic-book legend—only this isn't Captain Marvel. It's the new Marvel teen superhero . . . the Mighty Rebekah." Here, "Mighty Rebekah" refers to Rebekah Bruesehoff, who in 2018 at age twelve became a nationally known LGBTQ activist. When she successfully convinced the New Jersey state legislature to pass a pro-LGBTQ law, she did more than impress and inspire millions of people around the world. As Potter alludes to, she also caught the attention of the Walt Disney Company. Representatives of that entertainment giant contacted Rebekah and her parents and offered a deal too sweet to resist. They explained how they wanted to build an episode of their television series—*Marvel's Heroes Project*—around the teen and her recent success. That show highlights outstanding young people who manage to bring about change in their communities. Rebekah reacted in part by exclaiming, "It's wild to think the people at Marvel were creating a comic about me. It's like every kid's dream!"

Quoted in John Potter, "A Hero Rises: ELCA Teen Activist Inspires New Marvel Comic," Living Lutheran, March 19, 2020. www.livinglutheran.org.

to help others understand that God made you who you are, and God does not make mistakes."[46]

Coming Out to the Public

Still another tool in the LGBTQ activist's tool kit—and often a very effective one—has been influencing positive change through the arts and regular media. In this case, the most common approach has been for a young LGBTQ person who is well-known in the arts or entertainment fields to "come out" to the public early in that person's career. Older members of the LGBTQ community have done the same. A well-known example was in 2005 when *Star Trek* actor George Takei admitted to being gay at age sixty-eight. But this approach has tended to seem more genuine when younger celebrities do it.

The reason, according to experts at leading pro-LGBTQ organizations, is because those younger individuals seem confident in their gender identity or orientation. They therefore appear to be genuine, a quality that most people see as appealing. As a spokesperson for the HRC puts it, "Whether it's coming out as lesbian, gay, bisexual, transgender or queer, countless actors, athletes, musicians, politicians, TV personalities and influencers have helped advance the movement for equality."[47]

Among the many young celebrities who have come out publicly in recent years are singer and actor Miley Cyrus; singer and songwriter Tinashe; and actors Ian Alexander, Lili Reinhart, and Lachlan Watson. Reinhart, who is in her mid-twenties, earned notoriety for her work on the hit CW Network show *Riverdale*. She identifies as bisexual. When she began acting, she explains, there was never any doubt in her mind that she would be open and honest about her orientation.

Singer and actor Miley Cyrus is among many young celebrities who have come out as LGBTQ in recent years.

Moreover, Reinhart was aware that teen-oriented magazines and other popular media outlets that closely scrutinize celebrities would find out who she was dating at any given moment. So, it seemed sensible to get out in front of the issue of her sexuality so that no one could accuse her of trying to hide anything. She tells the online magazine *The Insider,* "I felt that since I've exclusively been in hetero[sexual] relationships, it would be too easy for any outsider, especially the media, to vilify me and accuse me of faking it to get attention. That's not something I wanted to deal with."[48]

Similarly, nineteen-year-old actor Ian Alexander, one of the stars of the Netflix series *The OA*, publicly identified himself as transgender at the start of his own career. Older relatives and friends told him about what LGBTQ actors in past generations went through—how if they wanted to make it in show business, they had to hide who they really were. So, he says he is grateful to be born into an era when that sort of hatred and discrimination is less common, at least in the business itself. Ian gives the example of going to auditions and seeing other LGBTQ actors who are also open about their sexual identities. Such a situation is highly emotionally affirming, he remarks: "I go into the audition room and I sit down and see other trans people and it's just such an incredible feeling to not walk into a room and feel alienated. I feel comforted to know that there are other trans actors like me and that I actually have competition. . . . I think that's incredible."[49]

> "I feel comforted to know that there are other trans actors like me."[49]
>
> —Ian Alexander, a trans actor

These words are hauntingly similar to those that young Gavin Grimm delivered to reporters after winning his fight for equal treatment under the law. The court's decision, he stated, was "an incredible affirmation for not just me, but for trans youth around the country." All LGBTQ students "should have what I was denied: The opportunity to be seen for who we are by our schools and our government."[50]

CHAPTER FOUR

Risks and Rights

On a June morning in 2011, the organizers of Chicago's annual gay pride parade entered a warehouse on South Halsted Street. Stored there were seventy-three beautifully decorated floats that had been created for the parade, which was scheduled to take place that day beginning at noon. In the weeks leading up to the event, as had occurred in previous years, various local anti-LGBTQ individuals and groups had expressed their displeasure. Being gay was disgusting and sinful, they said, and there was no place in decent society for such individuals to flaunt their depravity.

The parade organizers expected this sort of ignorance and bigotry, of course. But they also knew that such parades were perfectly legal. Attorneys at the ACLU, along with many other legal experts, had made it clear that marching in public peacefully to advocate for one's personal views or feelings is protected by the Constitution's First Amendment. That venerable American statute makes such displays a kind of free speech.

Nevertheless, when the organizers entered the warehouse, they had a rude awakening that reminded them that, legal or not, sometimes expressions of free speech have unpleasant consequences. The warehouse's owner, Chuck Huser, who was with the organizers, later recalled, "We came here at 5 o'clock this morning to start pulling [the floats] out to get them to the 12 o'clock parade and we walked into our warehouse and we noticed all the floats

People march in Chicago's LGBTQ Pride Parade in June 2018. The right to peacefully march in support of one's personal views or feelings is protected by the Constitution's First Amendment.

were leaning to one side. We looked and . . . every single [vehicle carrying a] float had a knife hole in two tires."[51]

    Wasting no time, the parade's organizers, aided by several volunteers, worked tirelessly to replace as many tires as they could before the event's starting time. Fortunately for the event's supporters, they managed to fix all but three of the more than seventy floats, and the parade went on without further ado. Meanwhile, Chicago's local office of the Anti-Defamation League (ADL), a group known for chronicling and denouncing hate crimes of all kinds, weighed in, saying that it "deplores these incidents, which may have been motivated by the perpetrators' animus [dislike] and bias against the gay community. We commend the quick and responsive work of the Chicago Police Department and strongly support its ongoing commitment to fully investigate potential hate crimes."[52]

Staging a School Walkout

As lawyers at the ADL, ACLU, and other organizations that fight for free speech and equality for all Americans knew full well, the incident with the gay pride parade floats was by no means an isolated one. It is quite common, they point out, for expressions of support for the LGBTQ community to be countered by negative reactions of various kinds. Sometimes the pushback takes the form of peaceful, legally protected protest against LGBTQ people. But other times, the reaction is illegal, destructive, or, on occasion, even lethal.

Thus, as many LGBTQ activists have learned the hard way, when they stand up for themselves there are sometimes unwanted consequences. In that regard, legal experts say, the way the activists respond to the pushback is crucial. For instance, ACLU attorneys regularly stress that activists be aware of both their and their opponents' legal rights and always act in legal, peaceful ways.

A clear example of LGBTQ individuals having to deal with the consequences of expressing themselves publicly occurred in February 2020 in Warwick, Rhode Island. To protest several recent incidents of anti-LGBTQ bullying and hate speech in the halls of Warwick High School, fourteen students staged a walkout. Some of them gay and some straight, the young people skipped lunch period and one class. Soon afterward, the editors of LNP Media, a Pennsylvania-based news group that was one of many media outlets that covered the event, issued a statement. "Silence in the face of bullying only strengthens the bullies," the statement read in part. "So we applaud the Warwick High School students who stood up for themselves and their fellow students last week."[53]

> "We applaud the Warwick High School students who stood up for themselves."[53]
> —The Editorial Board of LNP Media

The protesters were swiftly held accountable for their actions, however. School officials reacted by giving them in-school suspensions, specifically for missing a class without permission from the teacher or an administrator. The walkout's student organizer, Morgan Hackart, had determined in advance what was allowed and not allowed by law in Rhode Island's school systems. He had checked the school district's website and there had found that "although students are not disciplined for peaceful protests at Warwick, leaving class without permission and being out of an assigned area are disciplinary infractions."[54] This meant that students could not be punished for the protest itself; rather, the only penalty involved would be for missing class.

The Legal Aspects of Walking Out

Morgan and his classmates decided that accepting the penalty, which they viewed as minor, was worth getting their message across. He later called the in-school suspensions "lenient," and added, "I'm just glad there weren't repercussions for the act of walking out itself."[55] These legal aspects of the incident emphasize an important point for any students in any state who might contemplate staging a school-based protest. The ACLU cautions that students should always be aware of their school's rules and the punishments for breaking them. "The exact punishment you could face will vary by your school district,"[56] ACLU officials explain.

In Texas, for example, the local ACLU branch says, students considering staging a walkout to make a social statement should first look at local state laws concerning truancy from school. It used to be that in Texas, along with several other states, a student who skipped school could be arrested. However, the ACLU of Texas states that "Texas has decriminalized truancy, so if your walkout lasts more than three days or parts of days, you can't be arrested just for participating in a prolonged walkout."[57]

Nevertheless, school officials *can* discipline students for missing class for three days or more during a four-week period. Attorneys for the ACLU of Texas give this advice to student activists: "Find out the rules so you can tell if they are being applied differently when it comes to your walkout. If you are punished unfairly,

In March 2018 thousands of high school students participated in the National School Walkout to protest against gun violence. Depending on a school's policies, taking part in a walkout can carry penalties for missing class.

you and your parent/guardian have the right to make informal and formal complaints to your school district. Check out your student code of conduct for information about the complaint and grievance process."[58]

Online Posters Generate Heated Controversy

Another case involving consequences for pro-LGBTQ activities in a Texas school revolved not around students making personal political statements but rather a teacher doing so. The well-publicized incident occurred in August 2020 in Roma, Texas, and centered on courses at the local high school. The teacher in question was Taylor Lifka, who taught advanced English. As a result of the COVID-19 pandemic then raging across the country, in-person classes at the school were temporarily replaced by remote, or virtual, classes held via computers.

Lifka wanted to make the online experience for the students feel as much like a regular classroom session as possible. So, she dressed up the background of the visual images she posted for

The Right to Protest at School

Many American students do not know their legal rights in the areas of freedom of speech and the right to protest social issues at school. Attorneys at the ACLU often explain those rights on the group's websites. Responding to the question "Can my school discipline me for participating in a walkout?," the ACLU states,

> Yes. Because the law in most places requires students to go to school, schools can discipline you for missing class. But what they can't do is discipline you more harshly because of the political nature of or the message behind your action. The exact punishment you could face will vary by your state, school district, and school. Find out more by reading the policies of your school and school district. If you're planning to miss a class or two, look at the policy for unexcused absences. If you're considering missing several days, read about truancy. [Also] take a look at the policy for suspensions. In some states and districts, suspension is not an available punishment for unexcused absences. And nationwide, if you are facing a suspension of 10 days or more, you have a right to a formal process and can be represented by a lawyer.

American Civil Liberties Union of Texas, "Know Your Rights: Students' Free Speech Rights in Public Schools." www.aclutx.org.

her online course with collages of various posters that had long hung in her classroom at school. These collages included part of a Black Lives Matter poster and a rainbow flag. The latter is a universal symbol of LGBTQ people taking pride in who they are as individuals. Lifka placed a screenshot of those virtual classroom background images on her social media and waited for her students to check in and begin class.

One day before classes were set to begin, however, school administrators found out about her online classroom background images. They did not like her reference to LGBTQ people and Black Lives Matter, and a school official ordered her to remove the virtual posters. "My assistant principal told me, 'Please take the posters down,'" she later recalled. The veteran teacher felt that this request was unreasonable and refused, and later that day the school administration put her on paid leave. "I guess once that happened, I knew that it might be a rocky road," Lifka told a reporter for the *Texas Tribune*. "But considering being put on leave? I never really thought that that was going to be their first step."[59]

A few days later, the administrators decided to be more reasonable and told Lifka the posters could stay as long as they did not interfere with the learning process. But at that point she decided to make a firm statement about what she and many students then viewed as a degree of intolerance for LGBTQ and Black students in the school. Lifka told her bosses that she would not return unless the school system committed to instituting some new, fair policies designed to promote tolerance for LGBTQ and Black students.

While these negotiations were going on, suddenly everything "sort of exploded,"[60] Lifka later remembered. Someone in the local community sent a screenshot of the posters hanging in Lifka's virtual classroom to Marian Knowlton, a Republican running for the local district's seat in the Texas legislature. Knowlton promptly went on Facebook and claimed that the Roma school system was trying to turn its students into leftist radicals. Both the administration's placement of Lifka on paid leave and Knowlton's political accusations clearly show that even small attempts to promote tolerance for LGBTQ people can sometimes generate unexpected, negative reactions.

In Lifka's case, however, the critical pushback aimed at her also generated reactions of a different kind. In the weeks that followed, many thousands of outraged students, parents, and other Texas citizens wrote supportive emails, letters, and online comments and strongly protested the way the teacher had been treated. Moreover, an online petition signed by more than twenty-three thousand people demanded that she be reinstated immediately. This public pressure proved to be the deciding factor in the case. The school district soon reinstated Lifka and indicated that her posters could remain intact. The official statement read, in part, that the administration was "happy to have the opportunity to better understand Ms. Lifka's viewpoints and welcome Ms. Lifka back to the classroom. The district stands behind the concepts of equality and inclusivity."[61]

Laws Against "Promoting" LGBTQ Issues

In some respects, Lifka was fortunate that her protest occurred in a particular region of Texas in which the local community largely supports progressive ideas such as social inclusivity. If the events in question had occurred in another part of Texas, the outcome might have been different. This is because that state is among several in the country that have so-called no-promo-homo laws in place. Those statutes are specifically designed to prevent teachers from discussing LGBTQ history and issues in their classes. Some of the other states with such laws include Arizona, Louisiana, South Carolina, and Mississippi.

> "I was in an environment where I understood if people knew this 'awful' thing about me, I wouldn't be safe."[62]
>
> —Annabeth Mellon, a former Alabama high school student

A young Alabama woman named Annabeth Mellon, who graduated in 2019, recalls that while she was in high school, she felt that she had been adversely affected by the no-promo-homo laws in her state. Indeed, she experienced firsthand how those legislated rules can shut down attempts to talk about LGBTQ issues in school and make it easier for intolerant views to persist even if unstated. "I never had a [high school] teacher say being gay is wrong," says Mellon, who is now open about being bisexual. "But I was in an environment where I understood if people knew this 'awful' thing about me, I wouldn't be safe."[62]

Mellon recalls just such an incident occurring shortly after a guest speaker came to her sex education class. The speaker proceeded to talk openly about LGBTQ people and their needs and problems. "It blew my mind,"[63] Mellon says. At the time, she did not realize how unusual this was at her school and

The Need for Fair Treatment Is Vital

Although there are often consequences for instituting pro-LGBTQ policies in schools, various national organizations say that respect for and fair treatment of LGBTQ students in schools is vital. The reason is that numerous studies have revealed that young LGBTQ people continue to be insulted, harassed, bullied, and sometimes even physically abused in schools. GLSEN's eye-opening 2019 national survey found, for instance, that a majority of LGBTQ students were targets of anti-LGBTQ remarks at least once and usually on multiple occasions. Over 95 percent of those young people said they had heard mean-spirited homophobic taunts such as "dyke" and "faggot," and 54 percent said they heard such remarks often. Moreover, 26 percent of LGBTQ students said they had been pushed and shoved in the past year, and 11 percent reported being physically assaulted, including being kicked or injured with a weapon. Equally disturbing, about 57 percent of LGBTQ students who were harassed or assaulted said they did not report such incidents to school staff because they doubted that teachers or administrators would punish the perpetrators.

GLSEN, *The 2019 National School Climate Survey: The Experiences of Lesbian, Gay, Bisexual, Transgender, and Queer Youth in Our Nation's Schools.* New York: GLSEN, 2020. www.glsen.org.

---

hoped to hear more of what she viewed as enlightening, useful information.

To Mellon's major disappointment, however, that attempt to deal with LGBTQ issues in an open manner proved short-lived. Word of the guest speaker's frankness spread quickly, and the school administrators found out. They pointed to the state's no-promo-homo laws to ensure that such openness about LGBTQ topics did not recur anytime soon in the school's classes.

When Parents Make Demands

Pushback against attempts to be open in school about LGBTQ people and their issues can and does take other forms, and it is not confined to the United States. Only one of many recent examples took place in Birmingham, England, in 2019. Elementary schoolteacher Andrew Moffat, who had earlier won an award for outstanding work as an educator, wanted to introduce his students to the concept of homophobia.

The idea was first to define that concept. The teacher realized it had to be done in a very basic, nonexplicit manner on account of the students' tender age. After defining homophobia, he planned to explain that it was unfair and hurtful because it made some people "outsiders" with fewer rights and social support than the majority. There was no description whatsoever of what gay people do physically in the lesson, which Moffat called the No Outsiders program.

Almost immediately after the program kicked off, it came under fire from specific segments of the surrounding community. About four hundred parents, most of them conservative Muslims, complained. They also signed a petition that demanded that the new program be eliminated. Some of the parents even staged an in-person protest outside the school, carrying picket signs that read, variously, "Say No to Promoting of Homosexuality and LGBT Ways of Life to Our Children," "Stop Exploiting Children's Innocence," and "Education Not Indoctrination." The school administrators quickly caved to these demands and announced, "Up to the end of this term, we will not be delivering any No Outsiders lessons in our long-term year curriculum plan."[64]

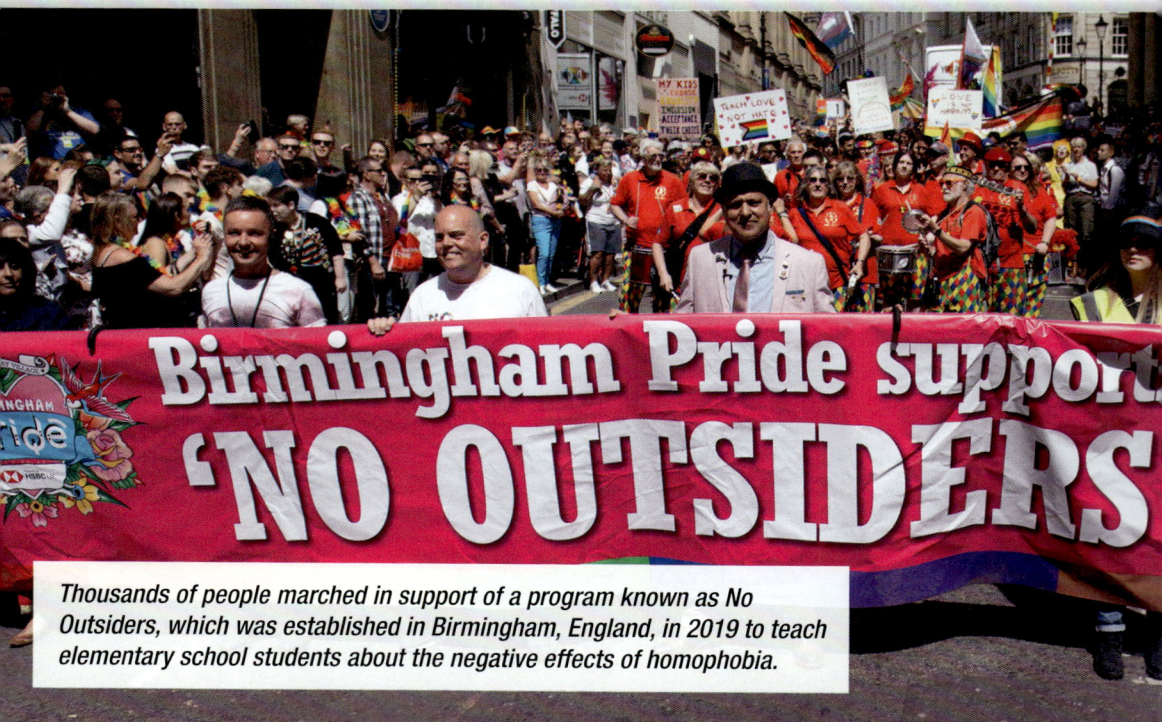

Thousands of people marched in support of a program known as No Outsiders, which was established in Birmingham, England, in 2019 to teach elementary school students about the negative effects of homophobia.

Positive Change over Time

Incidents like those in Birmingham, Roma, and Warwick underscore that instituting open discussions of LGBTQ issues in schools is often risky. School officials, parents, state legislators, and other members of society frequently object to such attempts to afford LGBTQ respect and equality. Vincent Pompei of the HRC and other experts point out that most teachers in the United States and other Western countries do desire to be inclusive of LGBTQ issues in their lessons. Nevertheless, Pompei states,

> "Educators [need] to know that their administration supports them and will have their back."[65]
>
> —Vincent Pompei, a member of the Human Rights Campaign

> Educators still have a tremendous amount of worry around LGBTQ inclusion. They fear parent or community pushback, and are uncertain if they'd be supported by school or district leadership if they took action. We say students need to see visible signs of a safe space, but educators also need to know that their administration supports them and will have their back if a parent or community member with anti-LGBTQ views complains.[65]

Despite the pushback Pompei cites, he and other experts are unanimous in their opinion that significant positive change in this area has occurred in recent years. And more constructive change in efforts to make schools more LGBTQ inclusive is expected to emerge over time. Each advance, no matter how small, the experts say, joins with others and collectively tends to move issues of equality and fairness forward. Ultimately, if a social cause is just, history has shown repeatedly that it is certain to prevail in the long run. For that reason, LGBTQ activists have repeatedly fallen back on a profound and moving phrase uttered by one of history's greatest social activists, Martin Luther King Jr. "The arc of the moral universe is long," he said, "but it bends toward justice."[66]

SOURCE NOTES

Introduction: Willing to Stand Up for Justice and Equality

1. Quoted in Lambda Legal, "Victory! Federal Court Rules Florida School Must Treat Transgender Students Equally Including Access to Restrooms," August 7, 2020. www.lambdalegal.org.
2. Quoted in Lambda Legal, "Victory!"
3. Quoted in Lambda Legal, "Victory!"
4. The Center, "What Is LGBTQ?" https://gaycenter.org.
5. Quoted in GLSEN, "Introducing the 2020–2021 GLSEN National Student Council Cohort," *GLSEN Blog*. www.glsen.org.
6. Quoted in GLSEN, "Introducing the 2020–2021 GLSEN National Student Council Cohort."

Chapter One: The Issue Is LGBTQ Rights

7. Mark, personal interview with the author, February 25, 2021.
8. Mark, interview.
9. Mark, interview.
10. Ella Schneiberg, "These Are the States Trying to Stop Trans Kids from Playing Sports," Human Rights Campaign, February 10, 2021. www.hrc.org.
11. Dhruv Khullar, "Stigma Against Gay People Can Be Deadly," *New York Times*, October 9, 2018. www.nytimes.com.
12. Khullar, "Stigma Against Gay People Can Be Deadly."
13. Khullar, "Stigma Against Gay People Can Be Deadly."
14. Quoted in Brooke Sopelsa, "Attorney General to LGBTQ Students: 'Bias Stems from Ignorance,'" NBC News, December 13, 2016. www.nbcnews.com.
15. Quoted in Sopelsa, "Attorney General to LGBTQ Students."
16. Mey Rude, "Report: Most LGBTQ+ Students Verbally Harassed in School," *Advocate*, October 20, 2020. www.advocate.com.
17. Shabab Ahmed Mirza and Frank J. Bewkes, "Secretary DeVos Is Failing to Protect the Civil Rights of LGBTQ Students," Center for American Progress, July 29, 2019. www.americanprogress.org.

18. Quoted in Clare Kenny, "LGBTQ Youth Share Their Stories, Offer Advice to Adults to End Bullying," GLAAD, October 18, 2018. www.glaad.org.
19. Quoted in Kenny, "LGBTQ Youth Share Their Stories, Offer Advice to Adults to End Bullying."
20. Quoted in Kenny, "LGBTQ Youth Share Their Stories, Offer Advice to Adults to End Bullying."

Chapter Two: The Activists

21. Quoted in Sam Levin, "'The Fight Doesn't Stop Here': What LGBTQ+ Advocates Want from a Biden Presidency," *The Guardian*, November 19, 2020. www.theguardian.com.
22. Quoted in Mikhaela Singleton, "K-12 Program Reaches Out to LGBTQ+ Students Across the Capital Region," News 10, December 18, 2019. www.news10.com.
23. Trevor Project, "Strategic Plan and Mission." www.thetrevorproject.org.
24. Quoted in Gerrad Hall, "How GLAAD Is Changing Hollywood's LGBTQ Narrative One Script at a Time," *Entertainment Weekly*, May 23, 2020. https://ew.com.
25. Ezra Morales, "I'm a Trans Student of Color. Supporting Me Means Fighting White Supremacy," *GLSEN Blog*, 2019. www.glsen.org.
26. Quoted in Mike Miller, "Julia Roberts Stands Behind Student Fighting for LGBTQ Rights Under Trump: 'I Want All Students to Feel Safe,'" *People*, April 29, 2017. https://people.com.
27. Quoted in Miller, "Julia Roberts Stands Behind Student Fighting for LGBTQ Rights Under Trump."
28. Rowan Little, "Here's What Happened When My School Listened to LGBTQ Youth," *GLSEN Blog*, 2019. www.glsen.org.
29. Quoted in Katy Steinmetz, "Beyond 'He' or 'She': The Changing Meaning of Gender and Sexuality," *Time*, March 16, 2017. https://time.com.
30. Little, "Here's What Happened When My School Listened to LGBTQ Youth."
31. Little, "Here's What Happened When My School Listened to LGBTQ Youth."

Chapter 3: The Teen Activist's Tool Kit

32. Quoted in Molly Longman, "Mental Health Care Is Crucial for Trans People—So Why Is It So Hard to Find?," Yahoo!, November 19, 2020. https://www.yahoo.com.

33. Quoted in Longman, "Mental Health Care Is Crucial for Trans People."
34. Quoted in Longman, "Mental Health Care Is Crucial for Trans People."
35. Quoted in GLSEN, "Introducing the 2020-2021 GLSEN National Student Council Cohort."
36. Longman, "Mental Health Care Is Crucial for Trans People."
37. Quoted in Disha Kumar, "Northview's GSA," *Messenger*, November 16, 2020. www.nhsmessenger.org.
38. Quoted in Kumar, "Northview's GSA."
39. Quoted in Kumar, "Northview's GSA."
40. Quoted in Jonece S. Dunigan, "Alabama Hate Crime Law Doesn't Protect LGBTQ Citizens," AL.com, February 17, 2019. www.al.com.
41. Quoted in Jessica Schneider and Devan Cole, "Federal Appeals Court Sides with Student in Virginia Transgender Bathroom Case," CNN, August 26, 2020. www.cnn.com.
42. Quoted in Tony Morrison, "Mighty Rebekah: Meet the 12-Year-Old Who's Changing How Others See Themselves in the World," *Good Morning America*, June 12, 2020. www.goodmorningamerica.com.
43. Quoted in Morrison, "Mighty Rebekah."
44. Quoted in Morrison, "Mighty Rebekah."
45. Quoted in Morrison, "Mighty Rebekah."
46. Quoted in John Potter, "A Hero Rises: ELCA Teen Activist Inspires New Marvel Comic," Living Lutheran, March 19, 2020. www.livinglutheran.org.
47. Human Rights Campaign, "Influencers and Celebrities Come Out for Equality in 2019," October 10, 2019. www.hrc.org.
48. Quoted in Frank Olito, "17 Celebrities Who Have Come Out as LGBTQ in 2020," *The Insider*, December 28, 2020. www.insider.com.
49. Quoted in Dino-Ray Ramos, "'The OA's Ian Alexander Is the Future of Trans Visibility in Hollywood," Deadline, April 2, 2019. https://deadline.com.
50. Quoted in Schneider and Cole, "Federal Appeals Court Sides with Student in Virginia Transgender Bathroom Case."

Chapter 4: Risks and Rights
51. Quoted in CBS Chicago, "Pride Parade Goes On Despite Vandalism of 51 Floats," June 26, 2011. https://chicago.cbslocal.com.
52. Quoted in Anti-Defamation League, "ADL Condemns Vandalism of Gay Pride Parade Floats; Applauds Chicago Police Department Investigation," June 27, 2011. www.adl.org.

53. LNP/LancasterOnline Editorial Board, "Warwick Students Protesting Anti-LGBT Bullying at School Have Their Voices Heard," LNP/LancasterOnline, February 18, 2020. https://lancasteronline.com.
54. Quoted in LNP/LancasterOnline Editorial Board, "Warwick Students Protesting Anti-LGBT Bullying at School Have Their Voices Heard."
55. Quoted in LNP/Lancaster Online Editorial Board, "Warwick Students Protesting Anti-LGBT Bullying at School Have Their Voices Heard."
56. American Civil Liberties Union of Texas, "Political and Free Speech in Schools." www.aclutx.org.
57. American Civil Liberties Union of Texas, "Political and Free Speech in Schools."
58. American Civil Liberties Union of Texas, "Political and Free Speech in Schools."
59. Quoted in Stacy Fernández, "A Texas Teacher Who Posted Black Lives Matter and LGBTQ Posters in Her Virtual Classroom Was Placed on Leave After Parents Complained," *Texas Tribune*, August 26, 2020. www.texastribune.org.
60. Quoted in Fernández, "A Texas Teacher Who Posted Black Lives Matter and LGBTQ Posters in Her Virtual Classroom Was Placed on Leave After Parents Complained."
61. Quoted in Joshua Rhett Miller, "Teacher Reinstated After Parents Complained About BLM, LGBTQ Classroom Posters," *New York Post*, August 28, 2020. https://nypost.com.
62. Quoted in John Paul Brammer, "'No Promo Homo' Laws Affect Millions of Students Across U.S.," NBC News, February 8, 2018. www.nbcnews.com.
63. Quoted in Brammer, "'No Promo Homo' Laws Affect Millions of Students Across U.S."
64. Quoted in Nazia Parveen, "Birmingham School Stops LGBT Lessons After Parents Protest," *The Guardian*, March 4, 2019. www.theguardian.com.
65. Quoted in Emelina Minero, "Schools Struggle to Support LGBTQ Students," Edutopia, April 19, 2018. www.edutopia.org.
66. Quoted in Pastor James, "The Arc of the Moral Universe," *Caffeinated Ramblings* (blog), First Church UCC, September 1, 2020. https://phoenixucc.org.

WHERE TO GO FOR IDEAS AND INSPIRATION

Books

Juno Dawson, *This Book Is Gay*. Naperville, IL: Sourcebooks Fire, 2021.

Jenny Kalvaitis and Kristen Whitson, *We Will Always Be Here: A Guide to Exploring and Understanding the History of LGBTQ+ Activism in Wisconsin*. Madison: Wisconsin Historical Society, 2021.

Skylar Kergil, *Before I Had the Words: On Being a Transgender Young Adult*. New York: Skyhorse, 2021.

Eric Rosswood and Kathleen Archambeau, *We Make It Better: The LGBTQ Community and Their Positive Contributions to Society*. Miami: Mango, 2019.

Robyn Ryle, *Throw Like a Girl, Cheer Like a Boy: The Evolution of Gender, Identity, and Race in Sports*. Ithaca, NY: Rowman and Littlefield, 2020.

Organizations and Other Websites

American Civil Liberties Union (ACLU)
www.aclu.org

The ACLU defends individual rights and liberties guaranteed by the Constitution and other laws. The organization's website features articles on student rights, free speech, LGBTQ rights, and more. Its website also provides ways of taking action at the local, state, and national levels.

Family Equality Council
www.familyequality.org

The Family Equality Council supports and represents the 3 million parents who are gay, bi, trans, and queer in the United States and their 6 million children. The website offers information on how ordinary people, both straight and LGBTQ, can combat anti-LGBTQ discrimination in their communities.

GLAAD
www.glaad.org

The website of this noted human rights organization includes the "Transgender FAQ" page that presents a well-written, informative general overview of transgenderism, explaining to teens and others the basic concepts, along with links to articles about related issues.

GLSEN
www.glsen.org

GLSEN is an organization devoted to ensuring that schools are safe spaces for LGBTQ youth. It supports teachers, administrators, and curricula that raise awareness of LGBTQ issues. Its website contains news articles and suggests ways to participate and advocate for change within schools.

GSA Network
www.gsanetwork.org

The organization's strategy is to fight for justice for LGBTQ people by empowering teens and others to educate the public on LGBTQ issues. Its website offers a hands-on tutorial of how young LGBTQ people can build their own local support networks.

Human Rights Campaign (HRC)
www.hrc.org

The HRC deals regularly and frankly with LGBTQ issues and problems. The site offers an array of links to articles that tell what is happening on the frontlines of the LGBTQ struggle for equality, broken down on a convenient, easy-to-access state-by-state basis.

National Center for Transgender Equality
http://transequality.org

The organization's mission is to help trans people enjoy equality and social justice, partly by educating politicians and other leaders about trans issues. Its website contains helpful information about how trans and other LGBTQ people can lobby their representatives in Congress.

Trevor Project
www.thetrevorproject.org

The Trevor Project is the leading national organization providing crisis intervention and suicide prevention services to LGBTQ people under the age of twenty-five. The website contains contact information for individuals and groups that can help LGBTQ youth in crisis.

News Articles

Amnesty International, "LGBTI Rights." www.amnesty.org.

The Center, "What Is LGBTQ?" https://gaycenter.org.

Kendra Gaunt, "How the Trevor Project Continues to Support LGBTQ Youth," *The Keyword* (blog), Google, September 30, 2020. https://blog.google.

GLSEN, "Introducing the 2020–2021 GLSEN National Student Council Cohort," *GLSEN Blog*. www.glsen.org.

Grace Hauck, "Anti-LGBT Hate Crimes Are Rising, the FBI Says," *USA Today*, June 28, 2019. www.usatoday.com.

Clare Kenny, "LGBTQ Youth Share Their Stories, Offer Advice to Adults to End Bullying," GLAAD, October 18, 2018. www.glaad.org.

Lambda Legal, "Victory! Federal Court Rules Florida School Must Treat Transgender Students Equally Including Access to Restrooms," August 7, 2020. www.lambdalegal.org.

LNP/LancasterOnline Editorial Board, "Warwick Students Protesting Anti-LGBT Bullying at School Have Their Voices Heard," LNP/LancasterOnline, February 18, 2020. https://lancasteronline.com.

Kara Lowe, "Queer Students Navigate Dating Scene," *Student Printz*, November 15, 2019. www.studentprintz.com.

Sarah McBride, "HRC Releases Annual Report on Epidemic of Anti-Transgender Violence," Human Rights Campaign, November 18, 2019. www.hrc.org.

Frank Olito, "17 Celebrities Who Have Come Out as LGBTQ in 2020," *The Insider*, December 28, 2020. www.insider.com.

Trevor Project, "Maloney Introduces LGBTQ Essential Data Act to Combat Deadly Violence Against LGBTQ Community," *Blog & Events*, June 13, 2019. www.thetrevorproject.org.

Dennis Velco, "97% of LGBTQ Students Experience Homophobia," OutBüro, October 15, 2020. https://outburo.com.

Gabby Weiss, "10 Awesome LGBTQ Organizations to Support," EveryAction, May 20, 2020. www.everyaction.com.

INDEX

Note: Boldface page numbers indicate illustrations.

activists and activism
  Gay Pride Parades
    Chicago, 41–42, **42**
    New York City, **24**
    violence against, 41–44
  organizations
    ADL, 42–43
    The Center, 5–6, 10
    GSAs, 31–33, **32**
    need for, 20
  protests against
    actions against supportive teachers, 47–48
    bullying, verbal and physical harassment in schools, 43–45
    gun violence, **45**
    teaching about LGBTQ issues, 50
  reasons for becoming, 18
  See also American Civil Liberties Union (ACLU); GLSEN (formerly the Gay, Lesbian, and Straight Education Network); Trevor Project, the
Adams, Drew, 4–5, **6**, 33–34
Alexander, Ian, 39, 40
American Civil Liberties Union (ACLU), 10
  ban on trans members in armed forces and, 26
  bathroom use by transgender youth, 34
  LGBTQ's constitutional right to march, 41, 43
  schools' rules and punishments for protesting, 44–45, 46
American Journal of Preventive Medicine, 16
Anti-Defamation League (ADL), 42–43
Arapaho tribe, 27
artificial intelligence (AI), 23

bathroom use by transgender youth, 4–5, 14, 33–34
Birmingham, England, 49–50, **50**
Black Lives Matter, 46
Blancaflor, Jaiden, 30
Bruesehoff, Jamie, 35
Bruesehoff, Rebekah, 34–38, **36**
Bucci-Mooney, Aryn, 19–20
bullying
  consequences of, 18
  extent of, in schools, 6, 16–17
  protests against, 43–45

California Association of Student Councils, 7
celebrities coming out, 38–40, **39**
Center, The, 5–6, 10
Center for American Progress, 9, 17
Cherokee Nation, 27
Cheyenne tribe, 27

Chicago Gay Pride Parade, 41–42, **42**
Collier-Moreno, Ethan, 7
Coming Out: A Handbook for LGBTQ Young People (Trevor Project), 23
court cases
  bathroom use, 5, 33–34
  same-sex marriage, 27
crisis hotlines, 20
Cyrus, Miley, 39, **39**

discrimination, 10
  consequences of, 17
  denial of basic rights, 13
  by health care providers, 8–9, **9**, 14
  ignorance and, 15–16
  laws in state
    anti-trans, proposed, 11
    no-promo-homo, 37, 48–49
  in schools, 6–7, 13
    bathroom use, 4–5, 14
    bullying, verbal and physical harassment, 6, 16–17
    sports teams, 10–11
  source of, 12
  types of mistreatment, 13
doctors, discrimination by, 8–9, **9**, 14

Ellis, Sarah Kate, 25

films and GLAAD, 24–25
First Amendment (US Constitution), 41
Fourteenth Amendment (US Constitution), 5

Gaunt, Kendra, 23
Gay Pride Parades
  Chicago, 41–42, **42**
  New York City, **24**
  violence against, 41–44
gender fluid people, 29
GLAAD (formerly Gay & Lesbian Alliance Against Defamation), 24–26
GLSEN (formerly the Gay, Lesbian, and Straight Education Network)
  extent of homophobia in schools, 16–17, 49
  National Student Council
    described, 19
    members, 27, 31, 32
Gray, Henry Roanhorse, 27
Grimm, Gavin, 34, 40
GSAs (Gay-Straight Alliances; Gender and Sexuality Alliances), 31–33, **32**

Hackart, Morgan, 44
harassment
  destruction of Gay Pride Parade floats, 41–42
  in schools
    actions against supportive teachers, 44–48
    against youth, 6, 16–17, 43–45, 49
health care providers, discrimination by, 8–9, **9**, 14
homophobia
  extent in schools of, 16–17
  and lack of understanding what being LGBTQ means, 15–16
  in media, 24
hormones, trans individuals' need for, 8–9, **9**
Human Rights Campaign (HRC), 10, 39
Huser, Chuck, 41–42

ignorance and discrimination, 15–16

Johnson, Miguel, 27–28
Johnson, Tae, 18
Journal of Counseling Psychology, 31

Khullar, Dhruv, 12–15
King, Martin Luther, Jr., 51
Knowlton, Marian, 47

Lecesne, Celeste, 20
LGBTQ
  meaning of acronym, 5–6
  myths about, 15
Lifka, Taylor, 45–48
Little, Rowan, 28–29, 33
LNP Media, 43
Longman, Molly, 31
Lynch, Loretta, 15–16

Manoj, Maansi, 32
Marvel's Heroes Project, 38
media and GLAAD, 24–25
Mellon, Annabeth, 48–49
mental health and same-sex marriage, 14–15
military, ban on LGBTQ people in, 10, 26
Moffat, Andrew, 49–50
Morales, Ezra, 26–27
Mota, Ashton, 35

Native Americans, 27
New Jersey, 34–38
New York City Gay Pride Parade, **24**
No Outsiders program, 49–50, **50**
no-promo-homo laws, 37, 48–49

Osage Citizens for Marriage Equality, 27

People (magazine), 27, 28

physical harassment in schools, 6, 16–17
Pompei, Vincent, 51
Potter, John, 38
Puga, Chuck, 35

queer, use of term, 5–6
Quilantan, Bianca, 11

Rajski, Peggy, 20, **21**
Reinhart, Lili, 39–40
Roberts, Julia, 28
Roma, Texas, 45–48
Rude, Mey, 16–17

Samelo, Eric, 32–33
same-sex marriage
  mental health and, 14–15
  Native American support for, 27
  US Supreme Court decision, 27
Schneiberg, Ella, 11
schools
  actions against supportive teachers in, 44–48
  bullying, verbal and physical harassment in, 6, 16–17
  extent of, 49
  protests against, 43–45
  discrimination against LGBTQ youth in
    bathroom use, 14
    sports teams and clubs, 10–11, 13
  discussion of LGBTQ issues in, 7, 37, 48–49
  effect of remote learning, 11
  extent of homophobia in, 6, 16–17
  fear of LGBTQ inclusion, 51
  GSAs in, 31–33, **32**
  working with administrators, 28–29, 35
Schwartz, Athena, 18

Silverman, Esmée, 14
Singareddy, Suraj, 31–32
social media, as support, 22–23, 30–31
social stigma, 12
South Dakota, 10–11
Stone, Randy, 20, **21**
suicide, 12
   increased, attempts due to discrimination, 17
   rate among LGBTQ youth, 22
   same-sex marriage and, 14–15
   Trevor Project and, 21

Takei, George, 38
television and GLAAD, 24–25
Texas, 44–48
Texas Tribune, 47
Tinashe, 39
transgender (trans) youth
   bathroom use by, 4–5, 14, 33–34
   gender mismatch between body and brain, 8
   hormone needs of, 8–9, **9**
   legislation against
      no-promo-homo laws, 37, 48–49
      proposed in states, 11
Trevor (film), 20
Trevor Project, the
   AI applications used by, 23
   establishment of, 20–21
   goal, 22
   handbook published by, 23
   participation in Gay Pride Parade, **24**
   remote learning and crisis support needs, 11
   suicide rate among LGBTQ youth, 22
   TrevorChat, 23
   Trevor Lifeline, 22, 24
   TrevorSpace, 22
   Trevor Youth Advisory Council, 23
Trump, Donald
   ban on LGBTQ people in military, 10, 26
   trans people's use of bathrooms and, 14

US Constitution
   equal protection clause, 5
   freedom of speech, 41
US Supreme Court, 27

verbal harassment, extent of, in schools, 16

Warwick High School, Rhode Island, 43–44

PICTURE CREDITS

Cover: paintings/Shutterstock.com

6: Associated Press
9: Octavio Jones/ZUMA Press/Newscom
13: Rawpixel.com/Shutterstock.com
17: tommaso79/Shutterstock.com
21: Associated Press
24: Lee Snider Photo Images/Shutterstock.com
28: Ingus Kruklitis/Shutterstock.com
32: Rawpixel.com/Shutterstock.com
36: Associated Press
39: Tinseltown/Shutterstock.com
42: Roberto Galan/Shutterstock.com
45: bakdc/Shutterstock.com
50: Katja Ogrin/ZUMA Press/Newscom

ABOUT THE AUTHOR

Classical historian and award-winning author Don Nardo has written numerous volumes about scientific and medical topics, including *Destined for Space* (winner of the Eugene M. Emme Award for best astronomical literature), *Tycho Brahe* (winner of the National Science Teaching Association's best book of the year), *The Science of Vaccines, Teens and Birth Control, Breast Cancer,* and *The History of Science.* Nardo, who also composes and arranges orchestral music, lives with his wife, Christine, in Massachusetts.

WITHDRAWN
Albert Carlton Cashiers
Community Library
PO Box 2127
Cashiers NC 28717